on blue felix paper

introduction by Sharon Doubiago

on blue felix paper

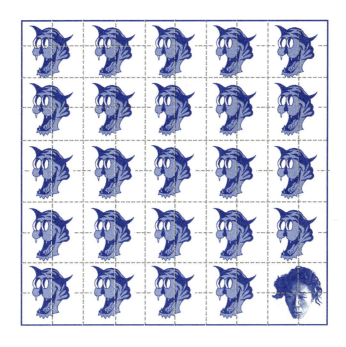

casey l.b. kwang

Acknowledgments

thanks to the West Wind Review for including "Us against theM" in their Sixteenth Anthology.

XOXOXO to Sharon Doubiago for the poetry in motion
thanks to Jonah for putt'n it togetha
to Doug at the door for running "Tales From the Town" at the Mark
to Gregory for boosting up the volume
to Jerry for the jump-start
to Andrew, Ed, and Bart for being literary mad addicts
to Gabriel for his curles, colors and attention to detail
to Jay-Hack for those long walks *home*
to Dorrian Laux for having smoke breaks in her poetry class
to Estin for his T'ai Chi kindness
to my buddy Holly for being so fucking cool
to Mahi for living so passionately
to Jenn for *one-thousand and one lives*
love to my parents who raised me, Ken and Wendy
the Bonsi family, the Mac Gowans, the Elberts, the Todds
to my sister Erin for loving so much
to my mother Chang Kyung Sook
and my brothers Matt, Josh, Chris (the Bonz)
and Kwang Chun my oldest brother who lives the immortal poem.

Published by Wellstone Press 1998

ISBN: 0-9647066-3-6

Printed in the United States of America

"you must sing to be found; when found, you must sing."

— *Li-Young Lee*

ContentS

III.

IV.

IntroductioN

It must have been May or June last year at a Wednesday night open mike at the Mark Anthony. It was late into the evening, many had performed, I was in serious conversation with a friend at the bar, when a young man began reciting poems from the stage. He was coming from a world I don't know or have much interest in, that of alcohol and drug addiction, of the boys in their twenties on the streets in the nineties wondering if they'll make it to their thirties — poems in which he's drunk, on a bad acid trip, anorexic with pneumonia, on the shitter, fucked and fucked up — but what was coming through was a mystifying, even beautiful wholeness. He was telling of hitting bottom in a way that is socially (not to mention legally) taboo. He was telling it with startling honesty, without justification (except in the shocking testimony of his language, imagery and rhythm), without guilt or even (seemingly) regret. He didn't try to explain or analyze why. He just vivified the experiences and you knew the seduction and you knew the danger and you knew the hell. Not in any way that glorified the experiences but not in a way that diminished the truth of them either. When he was finished I didn't take my eyes off him, though risking insult to my friend, as he made his way through the crowded dark room. The urge to tell him was stronger than my normal shyness. "You're a poet, the real thing. You got it, don't lose it. Nourish it." Then he was nearby, and I asked him the strangest question, after biting my tongue several times. "Who is your mother?" I must have understood on the psychic level this profound question in his life; he did not mention his mother. He talked mostly about poetry. I learned that he had taken Dorianne Laux's poetry writing class in Eugene. He spoke of Mark Doty's poetry in a way that only a poet can, with kinesthetic understanding of the coalescence of rhythm and meaning.

In August he took my "Autobiography of the Soul" workshop at the Ashland Writers' Conference, and wrote the poem here of his mother, and others. Ever since that first night I've tried to name the quality that Casey Kwang possesses. I mean the mysterious one beyond the obvious power of his poems, story, persona. Words like *authority, surety, maturity, stage presence, wisdom,* somehow miss the mark. I think of *shaman,* the one who has been torn apart, limb by limb, then put himself back together in order to come back to the community and tell us. The *shaman* comes back in love. But then hesitate, that I do what he doesn't: by use of such a term glorify or romanticize or otherwise make attractive the experience of Hell.

And now we have his book, *on blue felix paper.* "It's about getting lost on a walkabout," he says. "I'm talking about home in most of these poems. I'm planing on building a home in the 'First memorY' poem. *on blue felix paper* is searching for peace." Searching for Mnemosyne, who is Memory, the Mother of all the Muses. This is a story of one who suffered the 20th century disease of amnesia and therefore wanted to die. (At mid century we glorified this as *Rebel Without a Cause.*) Casey's mother is Chang Kyung Sook of Seoul who lost "four sons / in half a lifetime," probably because of his father. I love the tenderness of the love poems here, I love the depiction of Eugene, of the boys, the very lost boys, and the exquisite, extraordinary paintings, "each / watercolor of my soul."

The beauty and skill of the fourth section, poems written in and of discovery are the maturest. There's even a kiss from beyond the grave. This is a boy who hated being raised in Southern Oregon and so when we arrive "HomE" in the last poem, to "mt. Wagner from my bedroom window," and he's eager to live, we truly rejoice with him and want to live too.

This week I saw him perform again at the Poets of Ashland monthly open reading. Perform? Recite? Casey Kwang knows his poems "by heart" in the deepest oldest sense and meaning. He ended with one of his favorite poems, "YOU MUST SING" by Li-Young Lee. Afterwards I witnessed a man writer friend grab him and say my exact words from months ago. "You got it man!" And the unspoken urgency: don't ever reject the Muse again. She needs you.

—Sharon Doubiago
(December 24, 1997)

I.

First memorY

i'm standing in a crowd of abandoned children
i'm afraid but i don't know it because
i'm always afraid

my brother and i are balancing ourselves
on a pile of wooden planks
we are planning to build a *home*
with these boards that were torn down
these boards thrown behind the orphanage
leftover from an outhouse or a shed
that was no longer needed

my brother steps on a rusty nail
the nail pokes out the top of his foot
he starts to scream
i scream even louder
is my brother going to die?
who is going to take care of me?
i don't know who my father is
and my mother went somewhere
and never came back

the other orphans gather around
and stare at the two brothers
pinned
to what's been
torn down.

Our first step back homE

we sit on a concrete wall
outside the yogawan
a busy street of Seoul
bent at our knees

the traffic is a noisy zipper
endlessly mending and unmending
itself before us
"i wasn't ready for this"
passes his lips
and a tear
chases his words
i'm caught in the moment

the traffic passes by
without a sound
i feel the earth spinning
and twirling
dragging the moon behind

the tear that made a path to his chin
jumps
            off

and vanishes
in the darkness
of the wall's shadow

his memories
were not ready
to be revisited
after these long years
after these long years of pain
of knowing and not knowing
of remembering
and trying to forget
after these long years

this is no longer *home*
this has been his reason
for wanting to live
and wanting to die
this
was better left alone

we sit in silence
with our legs
tingling from dangling
he wipes his cheek
with his shoulder
erasing what's resurfacing

as the moment passed by
the traffic became
a hundred zippers
flipped like a switch
with a twitch of his head
my ears bend back
to where they belong
and together
we jump down
from the wall
taking
our first step
back *home.*

Visiting the raiN

standing on the balcony
of my mother's apartment
smoking a cigarette
i look
out into the smog filled city
buildings
as far as i can see
the noise of construction
and heavy traffic
drowns out
the song of the bird
and the laughter of a child

a small boy stands
in the window
of the apartment
across the street
although i can't hear him
i can see that he is dancing
clapping his hands
jumping around in the window

raindrops start to clink
like pennies in a piggy bank
the boy reaches out
to the rain
catching the clear coins
in his small hands
he continues to dance
and sing his song

i duck inside
to finish my smoke
my mother's house
has felt the rain
one thousand
times
before.

What's losT

my mothers eyes
grown sad
weighing down her entire body
Chang Kyung Sook
wanted nothing
from this world
but to raise
her children
she would lose four sons
in half a lifetime

she spends her days
in the crowded city of Seoul
without the memories
of motherhood
but with the thoughts
of what it could have been like

i know little details
of my mother
and of nothing
from before i was born
my father was out gambling
my mother's
life away
i feel
empty

perhaps
she has lost more
than her four boys
she has
in the heaviness
of her eyes
lost
her little girl.

II.

Sleeping iN

my alarm clock
went off
hours ago
and i'm still standing
in the doorway
of the dream world
begging
for one more spoonful of stars.

My first timE

i stare
at my reflection
in the darkness
of her bedroom window

i knock
on her window
and watch
my reflection
vibrate
in
and out
of focus.

This morninG

we got up early
and made love for breakfast
and then
i gave her a ride to work
on my bike
and this is what i want to remember
this early morning romance
as the sun
is about to rise
the streetlights
still on
this town
still sleeping
and it is just
Jenn and i
in the cold morning air
her arms
wrapped around my waist
her ear
pressed to my back
listening to my heartbeat
as i am peddling

this is what i want to remember
when it's time to go our separate ways
when our sand castle
that we have built
too close to the tide
melts into the ocean
i will remember
this morning
as perfect
as a seashell.

HeroinE

she came to class
as she always does
long winter coat
purse
poetry books
cheerfulness in her pockets
this is what she carries

today however
she brought raw materials
in her distant stare
this
is what she perhaps
always carries

i think of her butterflies
and the years it took
to prepare
for today's lesson plan
my hands tremble
i take a deep stuttering breath
as she begins class
with a poem
about heroes and heroine

but this isn't what today's
lesson plan is about

today
is about
a shattered childhood
domestic violence
incest
fathers
molesting their daughters
"belt buckles and cheekbones"

today is about

"a stubborn moon that trails the car all night
stays locked in the frame of the back window
no matter how many turns you take,
no matter how far you go."   *—Dorianne Laux*

the class gets intense
an energy collects
the walls are like huge magnets
that repel
i look to see how she is doing
for a second
there is a br eak in her voi ce
and tears in her eyes
old tears
that appear
to have always been there

and now
her voice
is a whisper
and she smiles
and because
she smiles
she has overcome
and her song has been sung.

Bukowski's barstool

i imagine
Charles Bukowski
in his prime
belly up to the bar
with bells on
blending in
with the barflies
and the blue collar boys
pounding pints of beer
pounding his life away
with one
after another

i imagine him with patience
at the end of each pint
his head tilted back
with one hand braced to the bar
the other hand
palming the pint to his lips
as he waits

patiently

for that bubbly back washed beer slug
to crawl out
from the bottom of each pint

i imagine
this is where a lot of his poems were lost
those surreal thoughts
that flashed
and then vanished
while waiting for that slug to slide
and i wonder about those poems
that never made it to his greasy typewriter
those poems
left behind

stuck to the bottom of barstools
like bubble gum

left behind for anyone
who wanted to reach down
and feel
the oddness
of it's shape.

Us against theM

all my life
it has been
us against them
us were the misfits
them were the normies
them couldn't drink like us
them had to get up in the morning
and work the nine to five
us worked the fourtwenty
them carried water bottles
and umbrellas
daily planners
and exact change
us carried, rock
weed
fungus
acid
fire
and Visine
them had Luke Skywalker
and Ward Cleaver on their side
them had Ranger Rick and Merry Poppins
with her spoon full of sugar
us had Bobba-Fett and Burroughs
the Merry Pranksters
and Alex
with his three droogs
Pete
Georgie
and Dim Dim
us were afraid to live
them were afraid to die
us were living it up
them were simply living
us went to the market and had roast beef
them stayed home
and had none

us didn't know for sure
and neither did them
us looked in the mirror
and saw them
looking at us
and them were afraid
just like us
and we all wanted to die
and go
wee wee wee
all the way *home*.

EugenE

eugene was my heaven and hell
it was in eugene that i felt the rain
like i had never felt rain before
piercing
calming
raging
soothing
down
down
down
it came
and came
and i couldn't escape it

waiting for the bus
riding my bike
walking to class
running from bar to bar
the rain was out to get me
out to change me
and it soaked me in eugene
washed me away until it left me
drenched
with an unwashable reality
it was pouring down rain
when i found me
in eugene.

DeaD

go to heaven Jerry, go to heaven
the long strange trip is over
and life goes on

the wildflowers in Eugene are blooming
and it's still raining on all the wrong days
some deadheads have been riding around
on skateboards
selling posters of you
and your magic guitar
an artist painted a mural of you
on the side of Circle K
vandals put a swastika on your forehead
this town hasn't changed much since you left
Eugene still hates you
and misses you

you know what we all could use?
yes, a miracle
maybe you could break bread with God and ask for one
ask God
to kill everyone for a day
we all could use an early taste of death
to replenish the essence of life itself
we need to get lost
so that we can find love in stranger places
like at the bottom a rainbow-snow-cone
or somewhere
in between
the hop
the skip
and the jump
or perhaps
exactly
in the absence of time
the miracle already happened
it's great to be dead.

ZeuS

the first day i saw
Zeus
he was walking down 13th
with dark rimmed glasses on
a bra on over his flannel
and a colander
on his head

he looked more pissed off
than mentally ill

and people fuck with him
on a daily basis
mostly frat boys
pretending like
he's their best friend

and i've heard
so many stories
about his story

ex-college professor
who eats barbie doll heads
a merry prankster
an electric cool-aid acid man
ate a bible and never came back

and why come back Zeus?
what would you want to do
now that you have unlearned
what we have learned

teach?

RavE

we walk to the warehouse
swarming with tweekers
and trippers
and trash can junkies   oh my
we die
with a quick lick of a fingertip
our bodies belong to techno
our minds go
we pass bowls
and share bodies in the dark
everything thumps and flashes
lasers on the walls
neon in our eyelids
sound is approximately six seconds behind
we feel electric
plugged in
lost and found
and this warehouse
has no absolutes
no reasoning
no direction
no beginning or end
but it all makes sense
and somehow
this warehouse
finds tomorrow
and tomorrow is so amazing
you crawl out of the rave cave
grinning
and picking flowers.

Boys night ouT

Bart and Brando
are on their way over
we'll be meeting some bastards
down at the bar
Floater is playing at John Henry's
when Floater's plugged in
i'm there to see it
but first things first
Chad and I are burning bowls
and drinking with Johnnie Walker

the clock steps
the bowls burn down
the clock stops

Johnnie Walker takes a hike through our veins

the clock jumps
the door knocks
Bart and Brando show up with bells on
Brando's got spikes on
it's boys night out
and whoever gets slamfucked and spundone the worst
wins
we walk to John Henry's
mr. dickhead is carding at the door
tonight the stamp that gets you in
is a screw
Floater is on stage and manic
the pit is amp'n
people are falling over
we're all stoned
wired
fried
and fuckt
we order red label and black
Jägger and Jack

Freddy Fudpuckers and Alien Secretions
around the horn
the crowd bumps half the booze
the other half is down the pike
we order again
we slam'em again
and now we're heading for the pit.

Rush houR

if you've ever been to Eugene
you'll remember the rain
i liked it best at 2:17
in the morning
my buddies and I
would ditch the bar
and head for Seven-Eleven
on campus

walking in the rain
drunk
at night
is magic
the black pavement and puddles
come alive
reflecting neon signs
and streetlights
our faces turn to porcelain
dampened by the rain
this
is the closest i come to crying

we make it to Seven-Eleven
our sneakers
squeak to the beer section
we grab enough to make us puke
or pass out
then we get in line
with all the other drunks
that aren't done drinking

i loved the way everyone looked
standing in line
their arms
full of booze
their hair
wet and sexy

their eyes
bloodshot from the bong
this is the hour
when the grin
becomes contagious
we buy our booze
and smokes
and then
head *home*
to write

Drunk haikU

our brown paper sacks
go clink, with our cigarettes
hissing at the rain.

Two forty-fivE

i wake up
dazed
my hair tangled
i'm still wearing yesterday
i drag ass to the bathroom
this is what i get
for drinking my meals

sitting on the shitter
praying
swearing
thinking about last night
instead of today
i'm not ready for today
i'm not done with yesterday
it's been years
since i've been ready
for today

last night i assume
was the same
what could have possibly happened
to keep last night
from blending in
with the years before?

was it fun?
it doesn't matter if it was fun
it's what i do these daze
wake up
get fuckt-up
and then fuck-off all day long
and this replaces fun

it's two-forty-five
and i have fifteen minutes
to wipe
do my homework

brush my teeth
take a shower
pay the bills
do laundry
eat
and get to work
but all i do is blow my nose
and i'm still late for work.

Dead end jobs
and the dope fiends that work'eM

we get to work late
hung over
and dope sick

our stomachs empty
our minds
full of worthless shit
we're mad-dogs
working
dead-end jobs

we limp around the restaurant
with our tongues
hanging out
everyone's looking shaggy
Brandon the dishwasher
is cruising the kitchen
stacking plates
rattling off
every punk rock song as he goes
we've never heard
the same song twice
and i asked him
how he remembers
so many lyrics
and he tells me
he stores it in his brain
where common sense
and morals
would have been

and that's why we get along so well
the dope sick dishwasher
the irie chefs
the pill poppin waitresses

we all have
an understanding
of the endurance it takes
to show up
day after day
to something
that feels like
sledgehammers
slapping at your soul.

DrunK

i come home drunk
around 3 or 4 or 5 a.m.
but never before two-thirty
last night i came home around 4
and had a six-pack-snack
waiting in the frig
i was already drunk
but i kept drinking
till knockout

almost knocked out
with the lights still on
i stare at a thumbtack
pinned to the wall
it's holding up absolutely nothing
but it appears to be holding up the entire wall
i moan to myself
to block out
the piercing sound of nothing
that buzzes especially loud
when drunk

silence is torture
sleep is an illusion

i wake up around 1 or 2 or 3
but never before noon
with the lights still on
my shoes still on
and my thumbtack is still
holding up the wall

a beer sits next to my bong
on my bedside table
the beer is half empty
last night i could have sworn
it was half full

i grab the beer
and like a pinball down the hall
i make it to the pisser
the burn of a long morning piss
is the only feeling i get these days
the only hint of relief
is when i'm consuming booze
or draining it from my body
if it's not one
or the other
i'm scattered

i finish my piss
finish my beer
light a cigarette
drink gallon of water
and the only thought in my head
is fuck breakfast.

Fuck iT

some days
i wake up
and i put on my fuck-it pants
my fuck-it shirt
and my fuck-it shoes and hat

these are the days
i have gorillas on my back
these are the days
i could easily take it back

the beershits
the hangovers
the insomnia
the physical
mental
and emotional drain
the six-pack hack
the oatmeal brain
the half-rack hack
and the heaver-feaver that comes with it

those were the days
and i want them back
for no particular reason.

Low self opinioN

a shield in one hand
a dagger in the other
war paint
across the cheeks
and down the nose and chin
a football helmet
spiked cleats with spurs
a bullet proof vest
and camouflage pants
driving into town
in a tank
walking down the street
without a sound
hoping
no one will notice
the fear
the shame
the hate
the low self opinion.

Seatbelt LSD

so i am sitting here
with my dick in my hand
trying to get an erection
i'm panicking
cause my dick won't work
i dropped acid six hours ago
and now i'm so numb
i can't find my pulse
so i'm convinced
that i've o.d.'d
and gone to hell
without my heartbeat
and without the ability
to squirt sperm

and what a humiliating way to die
death with his dick in his hand
didn't o.d.
but died of paranoia
heart failure
i can see headlines
the six o'clock news
talk shows
and the world is laughing at me
and i can't stand it
not for a minute
not for eternity
so i dial
911
then hang up
what am i thinking?
what was i going to say?
"i can't find my pulse
and my dick won't work
please send an ambulance."
no way
i sit on the floor

afraid to move
everything i pick up
turns into a weapon
nightmares bleed
from every thought
neon patterns everywhere
hieroglyphics
kanji
symbols
thin air is thick with neon sperm
i'm inside a microscope
i'm in a cinema i can't escape
can't leave
cause i'm already gone
so i sit here
in the middle of eternity
with paranoia
on my lap
like a snare drum
i'm trying not to flop around
i can't help it
i'm a fish on the desert floor
i can't help but flop
i'm in a barrel
rolling down a stairwell
like donkey kong
i'm in a sadistic video game
and i can feel
every boot that kicks me
my body jerks
someone is twisting the dial
changing the channels
and i lay here on the floor
riding out the bad trip
watching the show
twitching.

Apathy winS

LSD and automobiles
are invention that clash
but i'm at a time
in my life
where clash
is good
i'm lost
i've forgotten
who i am
my friends are the same way
no wonder why we like things
that take us somewhere else

so there we are
crammed in my Nissan
frying on acid
flying down the freeway at 90
to the next concert

there's this game we play
we never talk about it
but we're always playing it
it's called
whoever doesn't give a fuck wins
everyone who plays
loses
and whoever wins
usually
ends up dead.

On blue felix papeR
(for B.C.)

LSD twenty-five
on blue felix paper
it'll get you there
guaranteed
there is no guarantee
it will put you back
where you left off
it's not a sunshine hit
or a jesuschrist
blue felix is a joke
and you're the punch line
it's a bogus hit of your worst nightmare
and you've
volunteered
to be the victim
of this laughing cat
this cat will laugh you naked
laugh you fighting blackberry bushes
sixty miles from where you dropped
this cat will leave you curled up
in the fetal position
in a jail cell
bleeding
naked
feeling motherless
and laughed at
by a cat.

What's really going oN

i'm at Max's
shooting pool with my buddies
drinking beer
and eating popcorn
for dinner
the man at the bar
with the black hat
wants to unload some shrooms
our ears perk up
we're done playing pool
now we're walking to my buddies quad
cause he's got a scale

the man in the black hat
pulls out a freezer bag
full of twisties
he's like a chipmunk
with an acorn collection
we put what's for sale
on the scale
then we huddle around
and hold our breath
the digital numbers roll
like a slot machine
jackpot
we exhale
god-almighty
we don't have enough cash
we unload our pockets
flatten out the crumpled bills
count'em
stack'em
the black hat man
splits the bag
tonight
is a good night
for everyone

we trip
to the graveyard on campus
the moon is out
it looks infected
it looks fried
and before you know it
we're down by the river
watching the sunrise
the four of us
sitting on a log
laughing at ourselves
that's all we want to do
is laugh
and forget about
what's really going on

Andrew, Ed and I
and the black hat man
we're in our twenties
stumbling around in the 90's
wondering
if we're going to make it to our 30's
we're drinking forties
smoking fatties
and time
is measured
in little
plastic
baggies.

TokyO

time stands still
when your dry heaving
at some strange club
that never closes
in some strange country
i needed sleep
or death
more than anything

on the floor
with some nasty toilet
i needed somewhere else
to pass out

outside
i look for my date
no sign of Mad
just smokers smoking
and bumper to bumper taxis

i end up
on the sidewalk
passed out
next to a pile of puke
that looks like
a melted snowman

i wake up
on a bullet train
going
i don't know where
and that's how i spend my days
in and out of bathrooms
on
and off
of trains.

On the shitteR

she put three checks behind my name
one for interrupting the pledge of allegiance
one for chewing gum
and one for farting loudly
and i was sent to the principals office
and he sent me home
and i went to counseling
and to the dept. of mental health
and the juvenile delinquent home
and to community service
and then to the drug subculture
then to the dumpsters
the gutters
the alleys
the graveyards
the warehouses
basements
rooftops
train stations
and riverbeds
and somewhere between
fuckt and fuckt-up
i lost my soul
so i sit here
soulless
on the shitter
anorexic with pneumonia
shitting blood
coughing blood
with a bloody nose
dope sick off of crank
sweating booze
bloodshot from the bong
i'm hell bent and spent
ready to die
unable to cry
i can't even scream

when the demons come
i've made it
this is what i was looking for the whole time
right here
sitting on this shitter
a few heartbeats away from death
and if i wake up tomorrow
i'll believe
anything you say.

SurrendeR

wrapped in the horns of the goat
the demons rape my flesh
i hang in the face of hell
where time refuses to age
i stretch to reach unity
it is not there
i've sacrificed my heart and soul
to a brick well hell
i'm slamfuckt and spundone
the demons are winning
but have not won

i surrender.

III.

Rejecting the Muse

MotherlesS

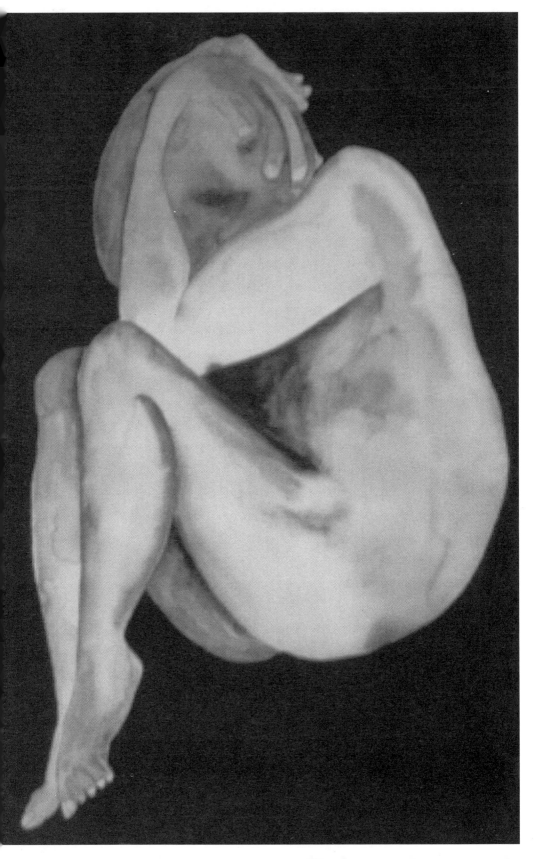

DualitY

Reveal

ResurfacinG

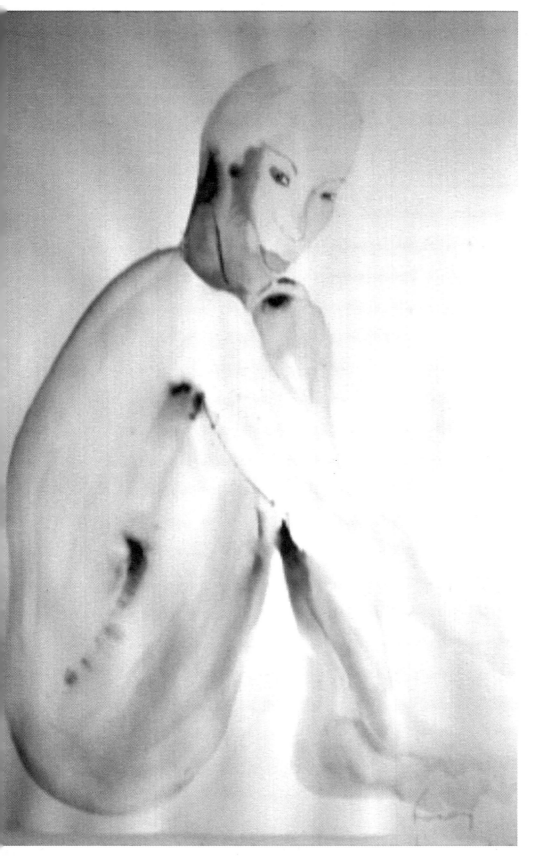

Searching for MnemosynE

Earthwomß

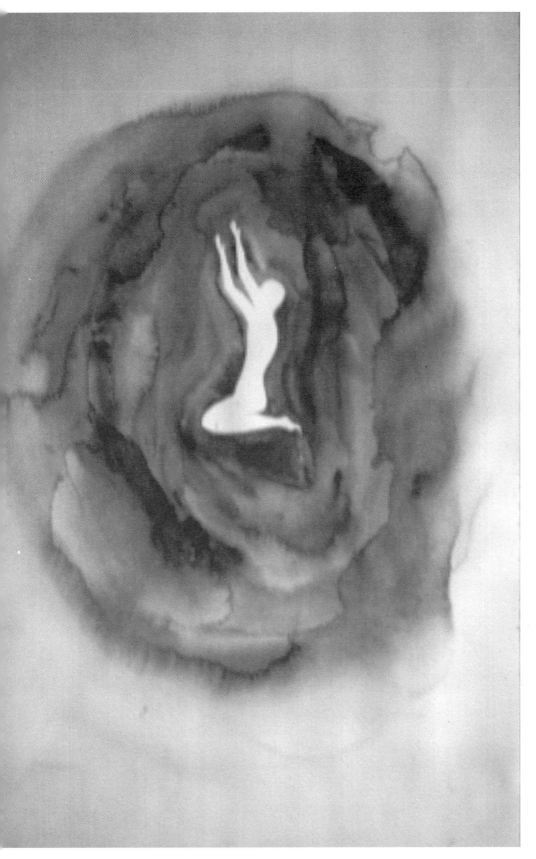

IV.

MoonlessnesS

the moth and the mosquitoes
are partying
in the porch-light tonight
a symphony of crickets
are exhausting
the only note they know
a small creature
is wrestling with darkness
beyond those bushes
and somewhere nearby
something
has triggered the skunk

this is tonight
this moment
with this moonless sky

the stars shine brighter
and this replaces the moon
this replaces that full circle of illusion
that sphere that appears flat

that circular mirror
covered in dust
and i wonder
whose face that is
reflecting
pale white
all scarred up
and worshipping
only darkness.

A one man plaY

last night
i dreamed
i was working in a chain gang
smashing stones with a pick axe
when the devil appeared
with a corpse

i dug a hole
and buried the body

later in the dream
i dug up the dead body
and took one last look at the face
and that's when i woke up

it's my face
i am the dead body
tricked by the devil
buried by my own two hands

to know me
is to place a foot
in the weightlessness
of my dreams
i'm about sins
addictions
imperfections
and fears

i am the devil in this dream
with something to hide

i am the dead body in this dream
possessed by the devil

i am the prisoner
the puppet in this dream

suppressed by the world around me
i am the world around me

and after dreams like this
i have
no more questions.

ClaritY

an icicle
melting
in the morning sun
is clarity

a crystal dagger
a work of art
a measurement of time
temperature
patience
brilliance

the dagger is solid
it is liquid
and it's leaving
it's returning to the puddle below

each drip dulls the dagger
each drip wiggles like a loose tooth
trying to hang on to the point
but slips
into flight
f
a
l
l
i
n
g
a sphere of liquid
full of light
capturing
the reflecting world surrounding
is clarity

the moment
in which

the world
contained
in a looking glass bead of light
is no longer a part of the dagger above
and not yet a part of the puddle below

it is that moment
when the world is separated
and in flight
to be examined
and then put back
to be whole
to be fluid
to be grounded once again

DrawN

back to the earth by
the vulnerability
of experience.

The poeM

the poem is pinned
to my passion like a tree
note and a jackknife.

Chapter siX

he looks back at the old road
it's hard to believe
how raggedy that road is
how noisy it's become
with the whirlwind of misery
howling down
those gutters that have grown like skyscrapers
that street
bottlenecks towards the back
here it's not much wider than shoulders
and the road
is full of pot holes and puddles
and you're always stepping
into something
endlessly searching
for those momentary orgasms
with the universe

he looks back at that old road
and realizes he is lost again
out here in the open field
he knows very little beyond
that raggedy road
he is willing to travel
once again
not knowing
but feeling
the cold air he breathes in
and feeling
the warm air that is blown out
and listening
in the background
to his heartbeat
strumming through his veins
like a rhythm guitar.

The way Elika moveS

she's the waitress
with a menu tucked beneath one arm
leaning into your smile
with her amber eyes
as she writes down
what you really want
and i've never been able to tell her
what i really want
haven't got the courage to tell her
i am in love with her every move

that the way she weaves between tables
on a busy thursday night
with her tray of ambrosia
is graceful to me
so graceful that it   deafens me
the restaurant goes silent
my friend keeps talking to me
but i am not there
i don't know where i am exactly
wanting
to be with her
is no place to stay forever
it's too hard on my heart
i have to let her know

the way her hair
slips out of her braid
and floats down
the sides of her face
leaves me   dangling
the way she tilts her head
glancing out the window
for a peak at the aching moon
is beautiful to me
so beautiful i must tell her

the way she holds up a newspaper
and studies it
standing
with her hip
locked to one side
her arms
extended
her hands in tiny fists
    crumples me
i must tell her

that day we went out to lunch
i wanted to reach
across the table
and weave my fingers
into her fingers
and see
if the palms of our hands
would fit into each other
like two halves
of something broken
i must tell her

the night my car broke down
and she walked by
as i was pushing my car
to the side
of the road
my heart was galloping
as she drove me home
i couldn't stop staring
at her eyes
her hair
her hands
and there is something
so precious
about her two front teeth
i must tell her

as she looked at

my paintings
on the wall
her body
curved towards each
watercolor of my soul
i had never felt so   exposed
i must tell her

i am in love
with her every move
so in love
i must tell her
to set me free.

MediocritY

i wake up
willing to give a shit
i'm somewhere in between
Fuck yeah! and Fuck it...
i eat breakfast
go to school
and then drive to work

and all day
i look
for magic along the way

and sometimes
it's as simple as
a rolled down window
on the highway
listening to the jefferson daily
daydreaming on my way to work
with the setting sun
reaching through the mountains
reaching across the orchards
to the highway
reaching into my window
to palm the side of my face
and to hold up my chin
with a single ray of sunlight.

MannequiN

i live by the highway
along the highway
is a supplies store
in front of the supplies store
there is a mannequin

she's trapped in a pose
sitting on a chair
her arm is extended
her hand is trying to wave
she's facing the cars
passing by

everyday she is trapped
in that same pose
sitting
waiting
looking
wanting a ride

everyday people fly by
without ever stopping
because she is not real
and everyday she is wearing
a different outfit
depending on the weather
sometimes a raincoat
sometimes a scarf and hat
sometimes a bikini
still, no one ever stops

it's just what happens
if you're plastic
and your face is painted on
and no matter what outfit we put on
our deepest desires
will fly on by

i pulled over one day
i got out of the car
and i gave her a hug
then
i whispered in her plastic ear.

Little brotheR

earth has great moments
but it can be vicious
on days you don't need it to be
many of us go through the motions of existing
without much fulfillment
some of us die this way
but some of us are constantly in awe of being
and many of us live this way

i'm just now getting to know mom
she's a tough woman who can endure
she's a trooper
you would have loved her tenacity
i think about having a little brother
having you
your face
mirroring moms perhaps
i would want you to have mom's eyes
although they are sad
they have allowed her to see what is important

america has treated me fair
there is a lot of freedom
but there is a lot of unnecessary confinement as well
lots of illusions
i've fallen in love
with the language here
it's music
if you speak from your soul
hey, ya wanna know
what my favorite word is?
it's onomatopoeia
click hiss buzz drip splish splash snap!

i spend most of my days with poems more than people
i guess i'm kind of a loner that way
big social gatherings make me
want to hide in the flower pot most of the time

i love those spontaneous cups of tea
on rooftops
with close friends
talking about pieces of the puzzle
with the heart to heart connection
and the laughter that seems so effortless

and this is what i would want to show you
moments
where love reveals itself
when guards are down
and our hearts
are like hats
on our heads.

HomE

I.
every two years
i visit my brother in Tokyo
i experience his world where business is war
and it saddens me
just like any other war
i watch people's faces as we ride the train
i wait for their expression   to change
but it's the same as it was two years ago
worn out from computer screens, deadlines, overtime
their wrist watches cutting off their circulation
the salary men jailed behind pinstripes
chocking on neckties
their souls locked up in black briefcases
the office ladies the O.L.'s
with their hair pulled back in tight knots
their high heels about to snap
their nylons wanting to run

at rush hour on the train
i'm squished between strange bodies
and we sweat into each other's clothes
how do they stay so polite in this WAR?

a cellular phone rings
everyone reaches for their handbag
their purse
their hip
as if they are looking for their gun
is it business?
or is it someone they love
wondering
when will they be *home?*

II.
home is dancing with the muse
it's fresh air
home is barefoot in the vineyards with a lover
it's the sound of birds in the wetlands
and the occasional burp of a frog
it's the mosaic of simplicity
waking up early to a kitchen full of sunlight
eating breakfast on the steps of the porch
with my daydreaming buddy Thunder, my cat
it's the view of mt. Wagner from my bedroom window
it's my roommate Mahi and his pumpkin patch in the
front yard
the morning glories along the fence
wild flowers and purple daisies.

it's coming *home* at night
looking out into the sky
and believing crickets are what stars sound like
home is peace
and every time
i go
to the other side of the world
or universe
or fence
or atom
what i find
i find
when i go *home*.

photo by Robert Jaffe

Born in Seoul, South Korea in 1974, Casey was adopted
at age four and was raised in Medford, Oregon. Casey
spends his summers visiting family in Korea and Japan.
He is currently a student at Southern Oregon University
and works as a sushi chef to pay for school. *On Blue Felix
Paper* is his first book of poetry and watercolors.